Letters From
MOOSE RUMP

By
Barbara Morgan
Illustrated by
Collie Parsons

AuthorHouse™ LLC
1663 Liberty Drive
Bloomington, IN 47403
www.authorhouse.com
Phone: 1-800-839-8640

Published by AuthorHouse 04/26/2014

ISBN: 978-1-4918-6787-7 (sc)
ISBN: 978-1-4969-0846-9 (e)

Library of Congress Control Number: 2014907731

authorHOUSE®

Introduction

Letters from Moose Rump is a compilation of stories that the author created while spending time on a small ranch in Oregon. The stories are in letter format, and they capture the real and imagined characteristics of "critters and things" that, in the author's mind, inhabited the premises of Moose Rump Ranch.

Inside the book, the reader will be introduced to Gypsy the cat and such critters as the Toad family, Elsa the cow, and Dirt Bag, the carpet. The reader will also find stories about Christmas, Thanksgiving, summer, winter, llamas and other characters that inhabit the canal, and a sumptuous meal made with Roadkill Helper.

The author does an excellent job of casting the subjects in lifelike form with unique characteristics and personalities, which, although they are totally fictional, make the critters seem real.

The stories in this book are engaging, and the book will find its way into the interest of a wide segment of the reader world. A teacher will find this book an excellent resource to calm the energies of restless children returning from recess. It will be a source of enjoyment as a bedtime story, and it would also be an easy find on a coffee table or interest centers in professional waiting rooms and more.

Will Work for Food

You are such a wonderful boy, and everyone who meets you thinks the same way I do. However, I want to remind you that when you start signing autographs at school, it might just possibly give you a "big head," and you will lose touch with reality. You will suddenly find yourself standing on the street corner with a sign that says "Will work for food!" If you have noticed when driving through the streets, there are lots of people who carry that sign.

If you would rather not even hold up a sign, you might want to consider eating at the mission; I hear it is really quite a good deal.

As you stand on the street corner with your sign, people will go by and throw a nickel in your little paper cup and say, "I can't believe that the boy came to this; why, it seems like only yesterday when his name was painted on America's Great Outhouse. His mother said if only he had studied his vocabulary instead of signing autographs, this would never have happened." His mother and father, of course, always throw in an extra dime whenever they pass him on the corner.

Whatever; here at Moose Rump Ranch, everyone is getting excited about the coming Christmas holidays, and no one could be more so than Gypsy. She has decorated the barn with Christmas balls, holly, many, many fish skeletons sprayed silver with red trim hanging on their noses, a tree trimmed with catnip berries, and a few gifts under the tree. Gypsy has a lot of cousins who come by frequently for a little hot catnip tea, and I can't believe how very formal she has been in having these little get-togethers with everyone. She's been serving such sweets as tea and scones, hot chocolate with glazed ants, and popped seeds of some sort.

Keep up the good cheer, remember we all love you, and say hello to all the barn people for me.

Christmas for the Moose Rump Ranch Animals

I felt rather sorry for Gypsy on this special Christmas Day. As you know, she has worked very hard to be a nicer cat to all the other animals, and she was really looking forward to a wonderful Christmas.

Anyway, at our Christmas Eve party, Prince Groundhog was passing gifts to everyone, and the tadpoles and quails were having a ball. Gifts were piling up around everyone except for Gypsy. Gypsy just sat there watching everyone get a gift, but none came for her. She decided she was being too impatient, and besides, all the gifts hadn't been handed out yet; but she also saw that many of the other animals had lots of presents—and Gypsy didn't have any. After the last gift had been passed out and there were still none for Gypsy, she just sat there smiling at everyone, trying to be brave, but she could feel the tears starting to come in her eyes. She quietly walked back to the barn alone and sat, staring at the corner, sniffing and trying not to cry.

I came in, knelt down beside Gypsy, patted her silky head, and told her I saw what had happened. I said it was just an oversight, that there were some packages that would come in the mail tomorrow and there was sure to be some for her. She said, "It's not that I have to have a present; it's just that it feels so awful when you are the only one who doesn't have any. If there had been one other animal, we could have felt sorry for each other, but there was no one else who could feel sorry for me—no one knows how awful it feels."

I told Gypsy, "You are wrong about that. I remember last Christmas and little Maria didn't get any presents when they were being handed out. Even though there were many gifts for her when we got home, it still hurt a lot at the time. As a matter of fact, I had that happen to me also, and it is a very hurtful situation no matter how hard you try to be brave."

But Maria and I learned a valuable lesson, which is that even though it really hurts at the moment, it will pass, and everything will work out all right. Remember, God joins us in everything we do, and things happen that are best, even if we don't know it at the time. Besides, Maria and I are very careful now to watch out for others who might be in the same jam. Speaking of jam, Gypsy suggested that we have a little jam on toast and some catnip tea—and we did! She sends her love!

" Elsa "

Elsa the Cow

How is one of the greatest boys in the world, who is, no doubt, very smart and even more importantly, very kind and always loves his family? Are you keeping up with all your important schoolwork, so that everyone will be able to say, "There goes a very smart boy"? When your family hears that, they will be proud to have a son like you.

Did you have a great Thanksgiving? The animals here in the yard sure had a feast. The magpies had row upon row of roast worm, well-rotted potatoes, and leftover spinach that Elsa the cow had not finished when she was last here. Everyone was assigned to bring something to the dinner. Elsa the cow got a little mixed up when she brought her pie; you see, she brought a cow pie, and she was supposed to bring a pumpkin pie. Elsa apologized and said she had thought a no-bake pie was the easiest to make, and the crust certainly had the perfect crunch.

Elsa is sometimes hard to take because she is so different. I remember last year when she was invited, she proceeded to eat all the cabbages, spinach, carrots, and at least a bale of hay, and all that was before anyone else had a chance to eat. Fortunately, the kids didn't mind that she ate the cabbages and spinach!

After all that, Elsa would burp up the food she had eaten and chew it all over again, and to make matters worse, when she was through eating, she began to clean her nose out with her tongue. Yep, she stuck it right up there. One thing about this is, she never has to use tissues or blow her nose, and besides that, she never has to sniff the snot right back up in her nose.

Yuck! That really puts me off my feed, because I can't believe snot would make an after-dinner treat for anyone. Another thing about Elsa is she doesn't speak English very well. She only speaks cow, and I don't know a single word in cow, unless of course you want to call *moo* a word. But what does that mean—hello?

Elsa loves everyone, and she is very kind and considerate. And even if she tends to eat everything on the table first, she gives a lot of good, delicious milk in return, which means ice cream, whipped cream, pudding … oh my, I could go on forever. Let's do lunch sometime soon.

America's Great Outhouse

How is the greatest boy in the world, who is no doubt very smart and handsome, and even more importantly, who is very kind and always watches out for his sisters and brothers?

Are you busy and good and working very hard? Are you keeping up with all your important schoolwork, so that everyone who sees you walking down the street will be able to say, "There goes a very smart boy, and I hear that he has always been a very smart boy"? And of course, Mom and Dad, sisters and brother will all sing songs about how smart you are, and how very modest and kind you are. My, my!

Now, I just know that you are still upset about not having a statue built of you and placed in the town square, where everyone could stand around and admire it, and having all the girls just go nuts over you. Now the thrill is all over, and you just can't cheer up; therefore, just for you, we painted your name on America's Great Outhouse. What more could you ask in this day and age—and it was cheap!

Between you, me, and Big Bertha, it looks pretty snazzy! I think Channel Zip is coming over this evening, so they can get it on tonight's news. The whole town is talking, and they consider it quite the nicest thing that anyone could do and wonder why don't more people do it. Frankly, I think that most people don't have a boy like you in their family; otherwise, that's all you would see in towns anymore, and surely the news would be quite dull if all you heard was that another name had been placed on America's Great Outhouse.

As I told your sisters, between garden parties and ant barbeques, this place is busy, busy, busy. I find that I can hardly keep up with all the goings-on. Many people might think life on this farm is a little strange, but believe me, everything that is written is true because it is written down. Or maybe everything is true when it is in a book or in the newspaper. Oh dear! I'm not really sure when something is true or not. What do you think?

Well, grandson, I must close now. We all love you a million, more or less!

Case of the Ruffled Feathers

All the critters have settled in, and everyone knows that Mr. Groundhog spent last winter in London. He finished his law degree, and the queen knighted him, so now we have to call him Sir Hog. He has a successful practice on the riverbank, and I understand that everyone seeks out his most excellent counsel. His first case came up just after he returned from London.

Speaking of law cases, it seems that the Toad boys were doing a little dance jig in preparation for a certain upcoming wedding, and one of the Toads accidentally kicked a tiny pebble and it hit Jim Magpie on the head. Jim fell to the ground on his back, screaming that he was dying, that he would never walk again and he was in terrible pain. Of course someone dialed 911, and the paramedics arrived and made a very careful inspection of Jim Magpie. They found nothing wrong other than a tiny, ruffled spot where the pebble had hit his feathers, and they told him that if he went to his tree and rested a few moments, he would be fit as a fiddle.

Well, that bit of advice didn't make sense to Jim, since he had no idea what a fiddle was, and if he did, he certainly didn't want to feel like one. He thought perhaps he should get a lawyer and make a little money out of this situation, because everyone knows the Toads make good money what with all the weddings they sing for. Why shouldn't he get some of it? After all, his emotions had been stretched to the limit, and he was feeling a whole lot of pain and suffering coming on because of the horrible blow he had sustained. Besides, just maybe those paramedics didn't know squat about first aid, and maybe he could sue them too and really get a lot of money.

Soon, every one of the magpies was following the now-limping Jim, who needed support from all of his friends just to walk. Wasn't it strange that Jim's leg was injured, when the pebble only hit a feather on his head? Why couldn't Jim remember which leg was injured, because sometimes he limped on his left and sometimes he limped on his right? It was all getting very confusing, but there is one thing for sure: Jim knew how to get down the lane to arrange for a big lawsuit against the Toads.

Now, Sir Hog had heard all that had happened, and he said to himself, "If I don't settle this case, the magpies will sue anyone for anything at the drop of a hat." So, after hearing the case, Sir Hog said, "I will require that the Toads pay Jim the amount of fourteen cents for his pain and suffering."

Purpose of Bathing

I heard a rumor that you might not be able to come to camp this year. Someone said it was because you were moving to Hawaii, since your parents probably won the lottery. Another said you were required to attend an important function with the president, and still others speculated that perhaps you decided to find another family. Of course that comment was met with much laughter, because who could find another family quite as odd as ours? Besides, other reunions might require that one has to bathe and brush their teeth fairly frequently, and what's the point in all that?

I personally believe that bathing all the time is quite a waste of time in most cases. I mean, of course, perhaps if one has mud all over him- or herself, or if he or she sweats all day long, it might be important, but if one does not stink, why bother? The skin rather resents so much scrubbing and raking all the time and simply feels terribly chafed if it is too frequent. Often, it will simply swell up, get red and itchy, and punish you for all your efforts.

I interviewed a few pigs on the neighbor's farm the other day and asked them how they felt about being clean. They looked up at me from their mud bath and acted as though I had rocks of the brain. They informed me that if they washed too often, their skin would burn to a crisp, and besides that, all their wonderful fragrance might disappear. Believe me, that smell doesn't just come on overnight; it takes a lot of time and work, and besides that, who wants to go around smelling like a bar of soap?

One pig, I believe his name was Roger, said he heard that people are talking about how you can't make a silk purse out of a pig's ears. Hello! Brain flash! The sky is really falling! What is all this about? I didn't get the logic in all this, so I dropped the subject.

In order to get back on the topic of bathing, I told Roger that cats certainly believe in bathing all the time, that at any given moment they could be seen washing themselves, and they wouldn't think of missing a single day. Roger said, "That may be so, but if you think that it makes cats so special, why do they go around using their tongues as washcloths and wind up with all that hair wrapped around their tonsils? And how on earth can you pick it off?" Yuck! Of course, Roger is right!

Gypsy Goes Skiing

Gypsy has been planning a great future in the world of skiing, or so she says. Also, she tries to be very nice and to treat others with kindness and courtesy; well, maybe not with mercy, but she is indeed kind. That is, as long as you are doing what she wants and having fun at the same time.

Yep! Gypsy has been having a lot of fun in the snow, and once when it snowed, she got so good at taking a big run at a small hill behind the barn, she could almost slide to the inside of the door on her bare paws. So she wanted to try some skis.

Now, for the life of me, I couldn't figure out how one could make skis for a cat, especially for a cat that isn't all that bright most of the time. Don't tell her I said it, because I will deny it. Besides, she is actually a bit brighter than the magpies that hang around here all the time. I asked the magpies the other day why they didn't head south for the winter, and they said it was too much fun playing tricks on Gypsy. I reminded them that Gypsy did have the last laugh during the fair, if they cared to remember.

One of the magpies still has his wing in a cast; not that it is still injured, it's just that he has a lot of autographs on it and doesn't want to spoil them by having old Doc Stork cut off the cast. Oh well, everyone to his own taste! Anyway, I was telling you about Gypsy wanting to ski. I did look for some skis, but the stores were out, so I had Papoo smooth out two small pieces of wood for her to use as skis.

Papoo personally thought it was rather a stupid thing to be doing with his time, and he really didn't think that Gypsy could handle skiing, but he did a fine job in making the skis. Sorry, I'm off track again. Anyway, Gypsy got on the skis by digging her nails into the wood and came flying down the hill like a house on fire, flew through the barn, and landed in a big pile of snow. I asked Gypsy why she didn't kick off her skis, and she said she licked them just before the ride and they froze to the wood. I poured some warm water on the wood and her paws came off fine. Gypsy just has to wash all the time! Go figure! She is such a vain creature!

Lava, lava, lava you!

16

The Mad Cat Killers

Things have been a bit quiet around here, what with all the feathered creatures going south for the winter. Just about the only ones left are Gypsy, some quails, and of course, those annoying magpies who Gypsy can hardly stand. Papoo felt sorry for her, so he went to the pound and picked up a small, calico mother cat.

After a week of quarreling, the cats decided to get along. They are trying to get used to the place, but it is so cold and snowy, they tend to just stay put in the barn where it is warm.

Your cousin was here for a week just after you guys left, and he was busy playing one of his Game Boys in the living room when the two outside cats got into a big name-calling, hair-pulling, nail-scratching fight with each other. They happened to bump into the door as they were doing it. Your cousin, thinking it was a murdering madman, jumped two feet in the air, his hair sprang out all over his head, and he came running into the bedroom yelling that someone was breaking in.

Papoo jumped up and looked out the window, and there were the two crabby cats standing very still in the snow. When your cousin screamed, it had scared them, and they thought there was a murdering madman ready to come out of the house and get them.

When they saw Papoo, they ran quickly to the barn, and I believe that's when the cats thought they might become friends after all, that it was probably the safest thing to do in case someone else came to murder them in their sleep.

So now we again have peace at Moose Rump, and the ranch gets very excited when it thinks of summertime and the kids who will come to camp and fish. Well, darling child, I need to close for now. Remember that we love, love, love you, forever and ever.

Gang at the Canal

How is the girl we love with all our hearts, and have you recovered from your vacation yet? How busy can everyone get? Also, the tests for school will be coming up, but that won't bother you any, because you are so very smart.

Well, the announcement came last night, and everyone is talking about it and planning a shower for guess who? Yes, it is for Martha Toad, and she is going to have a tadpole, or should I say tadpoles, because she is going to have about four of them. She said Doctor Stork himself wasn't exactly sure how many, but he did know that she was indeed expecting. Of course, Mr. Toad is thrilled and hopes he has some boys so that they can have a singing quartet down on the swamp. Of course, everyone knows that Toads have natural talent when it comes to singing.

The families who live in the garden always ask a Toad to sing at special events, and especially at weddings. Martha Toad herself usually declines to sing, because it makes her feel self-conscious to get up in front of a crowd. It seems she has rather a large wart on her nose, and although it is reasonably attractive, she hates it. She told me that all the women in her family have a wart on their noses, and there are some Toad friends who are actually a bit jealous and wish they had one on their noses. I heard one of Martha's friends talking about how her family tended to have rump warts, but never any on the nose, and wasn't Martha the lucky one? From what I hear, once the Toad family gets going on all this singing, they think they might make a record. If you want, I will watch out for the event and try to get you an autographed copy.

Well, my dearest child, I am anxious to hear from you about all those name ideas you are going to send for the Toad family. At present, we have to yell "Hey you" when we want to talk to one of them, and of course, every one of them comes a-running. There is no hurry, but when you have time, it will be nice to get your letter.

Let's go fishing sometime. We lava, lava, lava you!

Fall Fair

How does it feel to be with the big guys now? I'm sure you are taking the school by storm, because you are possibly the nicest and funniest kid there is. No doubt, homework is keeping you busy, so I'm sure there is never any time for mischief. Oh well, one has to give up something once in a while; however, I'm sure you get a little wink at the girls now and then.

Well, you simply aren't going to believe this, because I'm not sure if I do, but the rock gang and stick people decided to have a fair and rodeo this month in honor of fall. The stick people have volunteered to do the rodeo with wild cat riding, bareback sow-bug riding, the Rhode Island Red chicken race, the ant chuck wagon races, and a "catch the greased groundhog" contest.

Gypsy, of course, isn't going to be one of the wild cats being ridden; it will be two of her brothers and her four cousins. I understand no one has been able to stay on those cat brothers for more than fifteen seconds, so it looks like it's going to be quite a night. Apparently, the cats are famous for rearing straight up on their back feet, then putting their heads between their legs and rolling over. It dumps the riders every time: however, the Quail kids are pretty positive they can handle the cats. I hear that Duke Duck offered a hundred-dollar bill to anyone who can stay on for fifteen seconds.

Gypsy will be hosting the game of "knock the magpie off the fence." You get three chances for ten cents. You know how Gypsy feels about the magpies, and boy does she get a kick out of it when someone throws a good ball and sends the magpie off squawking with a few feathers missing. The last time one of the Toad boys threw a ball, it hit two magpies at once. Gypsy lost it! She was laughing so hard that tears were running down her cheeks. She had to close the game down until she had a chance to reapply her mascara. You know Gypsy; she can't stand anything that takes away from her appearance. Gypsy probably made more money in the fair than anyone else, mostly with the magpies; however, Big Bertha didn't do badly as the "fat lady." I swear, she is up to 375 pounds. She and her husband, T. W. RumpRoast, both look like they haven't missed many meals. They send you their fondest affections. Remember, we love you a ton!

Living-Room Gang

How is the nicest boy in the world? Have you been keeping busy learning to swim even better and keeping up on your schoolwork? You start public school soon, soon, soon! I can't believe that you are ready to start. You have grown up too fast, and Papoo and I want it to stop right this minute. Just stay the way you are. Of course, it might be hard on your neck to always be looking up at your friends, and it will be embarrassing to always be last when you are running, so on second thought, maybe you should just go ahead and keep growing—but not quite so fast!

I don't know about where you are, buddy, but it's been hot here. Nothing going on with the garden crowd, because it's too hot. Nothing going on downtown, because it's too hot, and we haven't even been fishing because it is too hot. Now that is hot! However, inside the house, it has been pretty nice what with the air conditioner and all. Sometimes I just sit around and listen to the furniture tell tales, especially Bud and Stud. They are the living-room recliner chairs. Bud has a big, handsome mustache, and Stud has a bright gold tooth in the front.

Sometimes they sit around and discuss what your cousin watches on the TV in the middle of the night or the games he plays. They think he is a pretty wonderful kid, but they always say their hearing seems to be greatly diminished after he leaves. Both Bud and Stud are rather stuck on Sophia, the sofa. They think she is a beautiful piece of work, even though she is a bit on the heavy side. Sophia says she gets her wide hips from her mother, that big hips run in the family and most of her sisters tip the scales at 250 to 300 pounds. They are what you might call "big mamas"!

Bud and Stud's favorite times are when the grandkids are here watching a really good TV program and eating popcorn. Sophia says her favorite time is when the kids fall asleep on her cushions; they are so nice and warm, and they make the house feel very good. I do know that the house is always especially happy when the grandchildren are here. Sometimes the house gets so excited that he shakes his roof and some of the shingles fall off. He looks forward to the fall, when there is a great big fire in the fireplace, the smell of turkey is coming from the oven, and we are all going over to your house for Thanksgiving dinner. Won't that be great!

Did you know that we lava, lava, lava you?

Papoo's New Glasses

My wonderful grandchildren, you are probably thinking of great times and discoveries yet to be made. You are probably sneaking a peek at the most handsome boy in school and praying that he has brains to go along with his good looks. And my other beautiful grandchild, you are probably still making plans for your upcoming wedding, because no matter what you say, the birds never lie! However, I just want to say that it might be wise to postpone marriage for another year or two.

By the way, I wanted to tell you girls about Papoo and his new glasses. I don't know if you are aware that Papoo can never find his glasses, so he will usually use mine. If he wears them for more than an hour, he will lay them down and then even I can't find them. So one day, I told Papoo, "You must buy some magnifying glasses at the drugstore so you don't have to use mine." So Papoo did. Unbeknownst to Papoo, he had bought women's glasses, with extra high-powered magnification. They had rose-colored rims with glittering, silver designs on both sides. When he put them on to show me, his eyes looked like two ostrich eggs with bulging pupils in the center. Sort of like a giant owl! I just smiled and said they were very nice.

The next day, after he had been reading for quite some time, he looked up at me and his large, bulging eyes were red and bloodshot. I said "My gosh! Ed, whatever is wrong with your eyes?" He said, "I don't know, but every time I read for a while, it feels like those glasses are sucking my eyeballs out of their sockets and yanking them across my nose."

It's so much fun to see him wear them, and when he walks with the glasses on, he has to feel along the walls to get to where he is going. Ding dong—try taking them off, Papoo! I should tell him what is wrong with his eyesight, but I think I'll just wait a little longer to explain the glasses to him. They are soooooo cute!

Guess what? We love you forever and forever—be good!

Charley the Spider

Gypsy the cat shared some information with me that I was sure you would be very interested in. She said that contrary to popular opinion, she personally hated eating mice, and after attending Toad's wedding, she decided to never do it again. Apparently, she developed a friendship with Miss Mouse, and they had such a wonderful time discussing recipes and ways to cook grubs, pan fry, and roast snails.

I decided then and there that when you kids come to visit, we will cook some of these recipes. However, I am going to draw the line on their sautéed flies; I don't even care if they put chocolate on it. A fly is a fly, and I won't eat even one! I don't even want to smell one.

Speaking of flies, our Charley the spider had quite an adventure yesterday. Charley had just made a fantastic web and was snoozing up high on the web waiting for a fly to come along for lunch, when lo and behold, Gypsy walked under the web. She stretched her back and paws and yawned, and her head banged into the web, pulling Charley down onto it. Gypsy started screaming, yelling, and twisting every which way to get Charley off her head; meanwhile, Charley was also screaming that the cat had gone crazy and they were all going to die.

Honestly, you simply wouldn't believe how loud and hysterical everyone was, and when he heard that entire ruckus, Papoo came running over with a big shovel, thinking that there was a bear loose. When he saw what was happening, he just stood there laughing, and he accidently dropped his shovel. Unfortunately, the shovel landed on his foot, and it hurt so bad that Papoo started dancing around on one foot. I finally calmed everyone down. Charley started to make a new web, Gypsy went to work on her recipes, and now Papoo is sitting in a chair with a big bandage on his toe.

Gypsy Looking Forward to Thanksgiving

Happy days are here! It is Thanksgiving month, and I can't think of anything but great-big dinners and desserts. What really put me in mind of food was watching the magpies enjoying a banquet on the fence. They had row upon row of roast leg of grasshoppers, well-rotted potatoes, and leftover spinach that Elsa the cow had not finished when last she was here. Some of the magpie dinner guests looked a little scraggly because they had been at the fair last month working with Gypsy and hadn't quite recovered from the slingshot ride she had prepared for them. Every time Gypsy walks around and sees one of the bedraggled birds, she starts snickering. As a matter of fact, right in the middle of the banquet, I saw Gypsy rolling on her back, holding her sides and laughing hysterically.

I told Gypsy that this behavior was not very nice, that it is Thanksgiving month and she should be in a more generous mood and be thankful for everything. Gypsy said she was indeed very thankful that she lived in a country where we didn't discriminate against certain birds just because they weren't quite so smart, that she was thankful there were no goofy dogs living in the neighborhood, and finally, that she had a nice home where she could heat up catnip tea when it was snowing outside.

I finally stopped Gypsy from her ranting and said, "It's all about this summer, when they bombed you with poop, isn't it?"

She said, "You bet your bottom dollar! It took me three months to get the smell out of my fur. I even tried washing in tomato juice, which guaranteed the smell would leave in two to four hours, but it didn't. I'm going to get those magpies one way or the other."

I said, "Wow! Gypsy, think about this: next month is Christmas; maybe your heart should be a little more forgiving." She looked puzzled for a minute, and then you could see a light go off in her head, and off she went to the barn. I peeked in a few hours later, and she was washing her beautiful coat, and humming "Silent Night," and I think that all might be forgiven.

Roadkill Helper

All the animals had a wonderful time here at Moose Rump Ranch during the Christmas season, except for Gypsy, and that was only for a brief time. She recovered from Christmas Eve and ended up with quite a few presents, including a new hunting knife.

She was so happy with the knife that she offered to help the magpies with their Christmas cooking. I told Gypsy to get a life, that magpies really preferred to peel their meals off the highway and eat them *au naturel* on the site. Nevertheless, Gypsy got several boxes of Betty Trucker's Roadkill Helper and convinced the magpies to bring their most recent roadkill to her. She mixed the kill with the helper, wrapped it in aluminum foil, and placed it on the manifold of Papoo's pickup to cook while he was driving into town.

Papoo was gone for several hours because he had a lot of stops to make. When he got home and walked into the house, he said he had a terrible odor coming out of his new pickup, and it seemed to be coming from under the hood. When Papoo opened the hood, I want to tell you there was the worst glob of garbage you have ever smelled or seen, dripping down the sides of the motor. Papoo was just about to get a hoe and a hose and clean it off, when down swooped about six magpies who grabbed the aluminum package and flew off into the field.

Later, you could hear them eating, slurping, and jostling for position, and afterward singing "For She's a Jolly Good Fellow" and slapping Gypsy heartily on her back, so I guess you could say the meal was a success. Honestly, I hate to criticize other creatures' dietary habits, but it's getting pretty bad when you think about what the magpies eat. Of course, you could bring up the dung beetle if you wanted to top the magpies. Go figure! Let's do lunch sometime!

The Llamas

You probably want to know about the critters living here in our new Moose Rump Ranch (besides the ones who followed us here.) The most interesting ones are the llamas. I saw them grazing out in a field right outside of town, and of course I just had to invite them over for a little fresh corn I picked from the field next door.

The thing I noticed right away is that llamas spend most of the time with their noses stuck very high in the air, and when they eat, their jaws go zig-zag instead of up and down. They are very well educated and usually don't care to hang around with the commoners, and if they hold their heads up high enough, most other animals hold back on speaking to them. Also, I heard that if they don't like your presence, they cough up a bunch of slimy spit and nail you with it. I have noticed that when you approach someone with their nose stuck up, the view is rather strange, and you are really not sure what you will discover should you continue to stare, so the best thing to do is look down, mumble something very intelligent, and walk on by.

Anyway, back to the llamas and the corn. Mrs. Juanita Llama, who appears to be in charge, said llamas didn't really care to eat anything that requires a lot of work, and anyone who knows anything knows that corn on the cob is work, especially if one has to eat their corn off the ground. The corn simply will not stay in one spot long enough to get your teeth around it.

If one is lucky enough to trap an ear of corn in a small, available hole, then eating some of it is possible, but then there is the problem of getting the cornhusks out of your teeth after you are through. It's not as though anyone has invented llama toothpicks, and strong sucking through your teeth seldom works (it usually just creates a lot of gas) Of course, llamas are not like horses, who just blast away no matter who is around, which proves that llamas really shouldn't hang around with just any kind of animal, because llamas are superior to all! Go figure!

We lava, lava, lava you!

Rules of Eating

How is the world treating you these days? Have you come to that stage in your life when you are thinking, "I really shouldn't be getting these strange, bizarre letters from my fading-fast grandmother?" You need to understand that every family has their weird members in it, and if you do understand that, then you can figure that someone will let them out of their cage sometime, and there goes all your dignity, because the day that family member escapes is the day you have planned for that special friend of yours.

Don't worry, though, Papoo and I have been practicing manners so when the time comes that we get to meet that certain someone, we will control all burping, slurping, sniffing, blowing, scratching, and picking. We might even shower, dress up, pop breath mints in, and brush our teeth. Now, who could ask for better manners?

Speaking of manners, how are yours coming? Have you had to eat at a very nice place where you are judged not so much on which fork to use, but how your plate looks while you are eating? As far as the fork is concerned, simply stated, a fork is pretty much a fork; it's whether most of the food you have just inserted into your mouth is gone and not clinging to the tines when you put the fork down!

Most of us pride ourselves on keeping our mouths closed while chewing and feel that is good enough in polite society; however, polite society also wants to be able to look at your plate without throwing up. This is where eating gets difficult, especially when you unwisely chose fried chicken, mashed potatoes, peas, and watermelon for dinner, all on the same plate.

I remember watching Papoo eating at a very fine restaurant, and he did very well when it came to chewing and using his fork. As a matter of fact, I was very proud of him, and then I looked down at his plate. My first thought was that he had just slaughtered a camel and was preparing it for the barbecue, and then I realized he was simply enjoying a lovely meal of roast beef, carrots, potatoes, and gravy. All of it combined into one luscious bite! Go figure!

So remember: good manners are very important, unless, of course, you marry the town lush, and in that case, just buy him a beer and forget dinner.

I Just Want to Be Me

So you want to make a lot of changes in your life? I say go for it! Meanwhile, I can only pray your tattoos are limited to your rear end, neck, wrist, chest, arms, and legs, because as you get a little older, they generally take on the appearances of moles, bruises, varicose veins, and leprosy. And of course, the worst and most embarrassing part is when you have *Martha* tattooed on your shoulder, and you end up marrying Bertha—oops.

Now about those piercings! So far, I have seen navel, eyebrow, all around the ears, nose, tongue, and all-over-the-lip piercings. The worst I have seen was the man who had screws through his lower lip in three places with the points pointing outward. First I thought, *My goodness, it must be hard for him to kiss his girlfriend.* But as I got closer, I didn't concern myself with that, because his face would sour milk.

Originally, piercing started out as a bone placed in a bored-out place somewhere on the face. I hear this is very popular in Africa, and it is certainly catching on here in the United States. Initially, Africans placed the bone in the lower lip, but every time they took a bite of food, the upper end of the bone went up the nose, and it turned out to be rather traumatic to remove. That led to the recommendations by many of the village shaman to put the bone through the nose. Of course, a bone with many years of snot accumulation can have an odd appearance, but isn't that the "I want to be different" look that all the kids want? Kind of like saying, "I just want to be me."

Piercing of the tongue has to be one of the greatest challenges in the piercing arena. If you interview some of the older pierced-tonguers, you will find that they tend to have chronic infections of the upper palate, cheeks, and tongue, along with most of the enamel scraped off their teeth. And of course there is the swallowing problem in all this—whoo, I think that one had a diamond in it, but not to worry, it should come out all right in the end—don't be too quick to flush! Sometimes it takes a little digging to find the tongue ring. I have known people who actually raise dung beetles for that very purpose. However, if you choose to do it yourself, I've heard that it's guaranteed to stop chronic nail-biting.

All I can say is, if it's not illegal—go for it!

The Kitchen Gang

What's going on with you all? It's been too hot around here for much excitement; as a matter of fact, it is so hot that I saw one of the magpies use a hot pad to pick a worm up from the ground. All the families here on the farm stay pretty much out of sight until the cool of the night, so I don't have much to say about them this month. Fortunately though, in the house it's cooler with the air conditioner, so right now we have a lot more activity.

I don't remember if I told you about Mr. Hardwood. He's the kitchen floor. Talk about a complainer—he gripes about everything and everyone, especially about Papoo, who we know never wipes his feet when he comes in. Mr. Hardwood says it simply messes up his entire appearance, and God only knows what kind of stuff Papoo wades through. The stench of it all gives Mr. Hardwood a headache and sometimes an upset stomach. You can always make him happy with a good mop scrub, so we oblige him every few days.

Mr. Hardwood's only friend is Westinghouse, the refrigerator, who was named after his grandfather, Sir William Westinghouse. Westinghouse is tall, and seems to be very arrogant, and is somewhat of a snob. He always has an expression on his face as though he smelled something very unpleasant. Maybe it's because he came from royalty and hates to live with the common people, especially right next to plump, jolly Tilly, the stove who laughs all the time and simply loves everybody and everything, especially when she is baking nice, thick apple pies in her oven.

Tilly's best friends are the kitchen-counter chairs. They are quadruplets, and their names are Prissie, Missie, Lissie, and Sissie, or as their parents say Priss, Miss, Liss, and Siss, who love nothing better than to have all the grandchildren sitting on them around the counter top eating, and talking about the fun things they are going to do while they are staying with us. When the grandchildren aren't here, the chairs get a little whiney and complain that there isn't anything fun to do, and they wish someone in this family would be kind enough to send for the grandkids, that is, if it's not too much trouble.

Remember, we love you forever!

Magpie Tries Piercing

How is the world treating you, young man, and are you ready for a great summer? Swimming, taking good care of your siblings, and helping mom is probably a good start. Did you know we love you a ton, and we are so very proud of you? Papoo and I love to attend your functions. We think you do an excellent job, and we know you have a marvelous voice. Someday you will forget that everyone is staring at you, and suddenly you will belt out a song and people will say, "My gosh, we didn't know he had a voice like that!" We will, of course, paint your name even larger on America's Great Outhouse and notify *The Enquirer*.

I bet you can hardly wait until you go to high school, and boy, will that be a challenge. How long? I suppose you will want to wear earrings, nose rings, tongue rings, and have a great chrysanthemum tattooed on your rump so you can be like the "in crowd."

It reminds me of the time when several of the magpies decided to go totally mod and have some piercing and tattooing done on themselves. One of the magpies decided to have a bull's-eye tattooed on his rump, which puts his IQ at about two or three. If I recollect correctly, it was Gypsy the cat who suggested that one. Needless to say, it took only about one hit with buckshot to convince that magpie to get the tattoo removed, and according to him, the pain went clear up into his beak and out his ears when they removed it.

Magpie said the pain was even worse than when the vet removed the pellets lodged in his bottom. He has walked very slowly and carefully and refuses to even think about sitting down. Also, the swelling has been very noticeable, especially with so many feathers having been removed! Looking at him puts most people off their feed right away. The vet says he will improve with time and the hot tub.

According to that magpie, the body piercing wasn't that bad, except for the first one. The brilliant magpie put the first ring through his upper and lower beak at the same time, and of course, he realized his error when he attempted to eat some particularly succulent roadkill the next day. Apparently, he lost several pounds by the time he figured out what he needed to do with the rings, and I believe he has sworn off all body piercing and tattoos. He said his body is just one mass of pain, and looking like everyone else suddenly lost all appeal. Go figure!

Well, buddy, remember, we love you.

Whom Should I Marry?

I don't know; you have looks, talent, poise, and a great number of pleasantries in your character. Who could ask for more? I am assuming that you spend a great deal of your day peeling the lovely ladies off your back or from around your neck. I presume that Mom is constantly trying to keep your ego in check, because she is afraid you will run off to Hollywood and stun the movie industry with your talent and skills and marry someone who you will love eternally, and of course you will only divorce her six months later and marry someone else that you will love eternally, and isn't it such a fun and dizzy life?

I think I heard a rumor not too long ago that your mom has chosen a very special person for you to marry in a couple of years. The gal already weighs in at about three hundred pounds, and I asked your mom why she picked out such a large woman for you. She said she didn't want you to be disappointed if you found a thin wife and then she started putting on weight every year and cried all the time because she was getting too fat, and since she inherited her hips from her mother, there is absolutely nothing she would be able to do about it.

The nice thing about being a big lady is that you will never complain about the cold all the time, and you don't have to share a three-person couch with anyone else. Since heavy ladies are always on a diet, you can save money on food, and of course your lady is one whom you will love eternally, and aren't you the luckiest boy in the world?

Actually, when I heard all that your mother had planned, I put in a call to Big Bertha because I heard that she had a girl about your age. The girl's name is Heloise and she currently holds the world's record in shot put. In all honesty, I didn't ask her what Heloise weighed, but it sounds like she is probably a little hefty, or perhaps she is very thin and has really big arms; either way, Bertha said she was very nice and that she thought you would like her a lot. If you are interested, she could send you her phone number, cell number, e-mail, and residential address right away.

I told her to go for it!

The Great Chicken Race

How are you, our sweet-natured, lovely child? Are you working hard on your schoolwork, and are you reading some really great books? I suppose you will be an absolute whiz in math and all other subjects as well.

As I told your sister and brother, you aren't going to believe this, but the gang around here decided to celebrate fall this year with a fair and rodeo. It was so exciting that I had difficulty waiting for it to begin.

The fair started Friday night with the Toad Boys singing "The Star-Spangled Banner" a cappella. I wish you could hear them sing. Talk about some nice baritone voices, and the tall, skinny one sings bass beautifully. They all have lookalike green suits and really cute hats with a feather. They also have bowed legs, which I think looks kind of funny, but all the girls yell and scream when the boys start to sing, so I guess legs aren't everything.

Mrs. Toad sometimes worries that the boys might become very vain, but so far, they don't seem to be. They are just really nice kids. They like the way God made them, especially when their knees stick out to the side the way they do. When they get to singing, they stand in one place and bounce up and down with the rhythm, which makes their legs go out to the side—interesting sight!

Also, one of my favorite events was the Rhode Island Red chicken races. We had fifty champions competing this year, and it definitely was the race of the year. Last year, it seemed that every few feet of racetrack, the chickens stopped to eat (you know how chickens love to cluck, scratch, and pick up bits of grain), so this year, we just stuffed all the chickens with grain before the race started.

So what did they do? The chickens laid an egg every few feet, and it took two hours for them to finish the race. However, everything worked out in the end because we all had scrambled eggs, fried eggs, omelets, hard-boiled eggs, barbecued eggs, eggs benedict, eggs on a stick, and egg sandwiches—all for free! Everyone went home stuffed and happy. Personally, I will pass on eggs for breakfast this week!

We love you more than you can guess in a million years.

Story of Split Ends

You are so beautiful, and surely you believe that, don't you? Well, you had better, because I have been writing all those things to you since you were little. And now that you are a young lady, you are even better, because there are going to be a lot of changes as you continue to grow and face all the challenges of teenagers in today's society.

Let's talk about your hair, which is so beautiful, soft, and silky-looking, and you take good care of it. But I'm not sure if you are aware of the danger of having such long, silky hair—it's split ends! I suppose you have been embarrassed at one time or the other when you passed some of your friends and heard them whisper, "Poor girl, she has split ends." But you see, this is not the real problem. The really serious problem is what happens to your eyes.

When teenage girls get bored, they will usually bend their head forward, run their fingers through their hair, select just one strand, and examine it very closely to determine if it has a split end, all the while saying under their breath, "Oh please, God, don't let there be a split end." If there is a split end, then it forces the poor, miserable girl to begin a complete head search to see just how many split ends she may have.

Now, this is where the real problem comes to light. You see, when one intensely examines a single strand of hair, she forces her eyes to become a magnifying glass. The result of all this is that one eye will eventually become exhausted and start to lean over to the other eye that is still working, probably thinking if they work out of the same socket, they can do a better job.

Some scientists believe that eventually, just as we lost our tails because we didn't need them, we will soon lose our extra eye socket. Isn't all that wonderful? If we wait long enough, we will end up perfect, and who knows, we might even end up without split ends, and wouldn't that be the miracle of miracles?

Monkey Who Fell Out of the Tree

Did you hear about the monkey in the local zoo who fell out of a tree and badly injured his tail, probably because he fell on something sharp? Anyway, the vet had to put eighteen stitches in his tail and told him not to be swinging around in the trees for about a month. Of course, the monkey is very unhappy—or more specifically, embarrassed—because he fell out of a tree, like who has he ever known in his family who fell out of a tree?

Being embarrassed is so hard to handle, because you don't know who to talk to that does not bring up the subject, and all you want to do is forget it happened. The most common questions they ask are "How did it happen?" or the best one of all, "Did it hurt?"

Of course, all one can hope for is that word doesn't get around so that perfect strangers come up to you and say "Are you the monkey who fell out of the tree? Do other members of your family fall out of trees also? Who is your father? Do I know your mother? Where did you come from? Didn't they have trees where you grew up?" Poor monkey, not only are all the animals laughing about it, but now he can't even swing through the trees to get away from it all, and besides, his tail is hurting about now.

I asked Gypsy the cat if she had ever known a monkey to fall out of a tree and she said no, but she had seen those stupid magpies fly around in the sky and slam into one another, and also she had seen the stupid dog down the lane chasing a car, and when the car stopped, the dog smashed his nose into the rear end.

Of course, this caused Gypsy to laugh hysterically, and it took her a moment to compose herself. I asked Gypsy if she ever did something foolish like that and she glared at me and said, "Of course not!"

Remember, we lava, lava, lava you forever!

Gypsy and the Fox

Our lovely child, how beautiful you are, and everyone here thinks so, and I'm sure everyone in town thinks so, and the angels in heaven know so! But you aren't vain, and you never think too much of yourself because mostly you are interested in everyone else, and *that* is what is so special about you.

Things have been rather quiet here at Moose Rump Ranch, since most of the residents are either in the South or hibernating underground until spring. However, we did have a surprise visitor last week. It was a big, red fox, and my, was he ever handsome. I believe he knew that he was, from the way he walked.

While he was strolling across the field, Gypsy was sitting on the railing of the porch watching him, muttering about how too many others kept moving in and how was the cat food going to hold out, and the Lord only knew what disaster might occur and everyone could end up starving to death.

As Gypsy was watching the fox, he looked up and winked. Of course, Gypsy lost all composure, and when she is a bit flustered or embarrassed, she will begin to wash her face, apply her eye shadow, and she pretended she hadn't seen him at all. The fox stopped and looked her way again, and all of a sudden, he smiled and shouted, "Boo!"

Gypsy was so completely shocked that she fell off the railing and plummeted to the floor in a dead faint. I ran out and started fanning Gypsy's face and asking her if she was all right. She stood up and said, "Well, I never," and walked off the porch with her tail and nose straight up in the air. I guess she was a little embarrassed, because cats really shouldn't be falling off rails or fainting.

As she walked away in a huff, I yelled at her and said I hoped she would have pleasant dreams tonight and think only about fun things to do. Of course, I'm always suspicious of Gypsy as to what things she considers pleasant, because revenge is ever on her mind.

Going to the Dentist

I just got back from the dentist, and honestly, I don't mind having work done anywhere the doctor thinks I need it, but one thing I hate is when the dentist says, "Open wide, this isn't going to hurt." Whenever I hear that command, my knees turn to jelly, my stomach starts to rumble, my heart goes hippity-hop, and my head starts to ache.

I believe that when God gave me a mouth, He meant it only to hold my teeth, store my tongue, to talk, and to chew my food. I don't recall anywhere it says open your mouth wide so the dentist can pick at your teeth and scrape your gums while his assistant sprays cold water in your mouth, sucks it up with a vacuum cleaner, and then blows icy air on your gums again.

Now, I will be the first to recommend that we all take care of our teeth, but consider the animals. Have you ever met a cat who complained that her teeth were getting dull and she wanted them cleaned and whitened? I have heard that cows sometimes complain that they only have one set of teeth, and they wonder why they can't have both uppers and lowers. Elsa the cow told me that the world just doesn't know how bothersome it is to pull the grass up with your tongue, grind it down with one set of teeth, and swallow it. Then one must burp it up again and again and chew some more so it will go through all the stomachs, and doesn't all that re-chewing just make one's stools so terribly loose. How humiliating!

I remember once, when I was at a zoo, I saw this huge camel standing by the fence. He looked at me, hoping that I would produce a little something sweet for him to eat, and as he stood there, he opened his mouth and gave a huge yawn, and you could see all his teeth. They were huge and such a fine shade of yellow and green with some brown. The other camels were among the first to state that those teeth were top-of-the-line, as camel teeth go. However, when he gave an exceptionally grand burp and exhaled right into my face, my hair went limp. As I recall, I had to shampoo my hair a number of times before I could get the smell out of it. However, I'm not blaming his teeth, I think it was his stomach—he must eat too much gassy food!

Dirt Bag

As I was vacuuming Dirt Bag this morning—Dirt Bag is my carpet, but I usually call him Dirt for short—anyway, as I was vacuuming Dirt, I was thinking of you when all of a sudden I felt this rumbling at my feet, which usually means Dirt has something to say. I can tell it's him because his rumbling is usually laughter and it tickles my feet.

The first time Dirt ever said anything to me, you could have peeled me off the ceiling, because it is not every day you have a conversation with a carpet. Maybe it's because I gave him a name that he decided to share an occasional bit of wisdom with me.

You can certainly believe Dirt knows what's going on, at least in this house, since he is awake day and night and listens to everyone's conversations. He is in charge of house security around here. He once said that he had worked for the DBBI (Dirt Bag Bureau of Investigation) before he came to live in our house and that it was his responsibility to keep track of everything that goes on, but not to disclose everything unless absolutely necessary.

Whatever; we have frequent chats, and he always keeps me informed about things that go on, but he never tells me secrets about the grandchildren, although he has been known to tattle on Papoo occasionally.

Mostly, my sweet grandchild, what I was thinking of is how you smile at people, how you are not afraid to say hello even if you don't know them, and although you had nothing to do with it, you are quite beautiful! God took care of the looks, and you are using the talents He gave you very well. Your cousins think you are quite the wonderful person, and so do Papoo and I! And that's what I was thinking about this morning.

It is true that Dirt can talk because I'm writing it down, and everyone knows that if something is written down, it is true, or is it if it is in a book, or if it is in a newspaper? Oh dear! I'm not really sure when something is really true or not; what do you think? I know one thing that is true: we love you and we thank God that He has allowed us to be your grandparents. I will write again, and don't worry, I really will because Dirt won't let me forget.

Gypsy and the Poop

Just wanted to write and let you know some of the incredible, exciting things that happen here at Moose Rump Ranch. Today was rather unusual, because Gypsy has been quite put-out most of the afternoon. It seems that one of the magpies was flying overhead and, completely innocent of any wrongdoing, dropped a little poop on Gypsy's head. You know how Gypsy feels about her fur; I mean, if the least little thing is on her fur, she sits for an hour cleaning it up, so you can imagine how she must have felt when that poop landed on her.

She came up to the door yowling loudly so I would open it, and instead of saying anything at all, she just sat there glaring at me with that poop on top of her head. She acted as though it was all my fault and wanted to know what I was going to do about it. Personally, if it was left up to me, I wouldn't have touched her with a ten-foot pole, but as luck would have it, Gypsy had an important engagement with some out-of-towners, and I said I would help her out. I suggested that she stand out on the driveway and let me squirt her with some water.

Of course that idea went over like a lead balloon. What a spoilsport she is—would you believe that she wanted me to get some warm water and a soft rag and clean it off of her head? We argued over this for about a half hour, when suddenly another magpie flew over yelling something about a great party occurring in the field. Gypsy ran off, saying enough was enough and that maybe she could find help elsewhere.

I haven't seen her since, but I do know she was entertaining her guests until quite late last night, and between you and me, I think they got into the catnip, because they were getting a little loud, so we can safely assume that Gypsy did remove that poop! Whatever!

About bird poop: the fact is—and let's get real here—birds don't have bathrooms, and birds don't know when they are going to poop. They just let it go, although I sometimes suspect they make a deliberate attempt to hold off long enough to nail some specific passerby.

Try going to Sea World sometime. When you get up to leave your seat, those seagulls fly overhead, indiscriminately bombing whomever it may concern. It's quite an experience; umbrellas are handy things to take with you. Also, have a really good shampoo with you when you get to your room.

Printed in the United States
By Bookmasters